HOW TO SAVE A SUPERHERO

CARYL HART & ED EAVES

SIMON AND SCHUSTER
London New York Sydney Toronto New Delhi

I love doing jigsaws, and this Astroman one is my favourite.

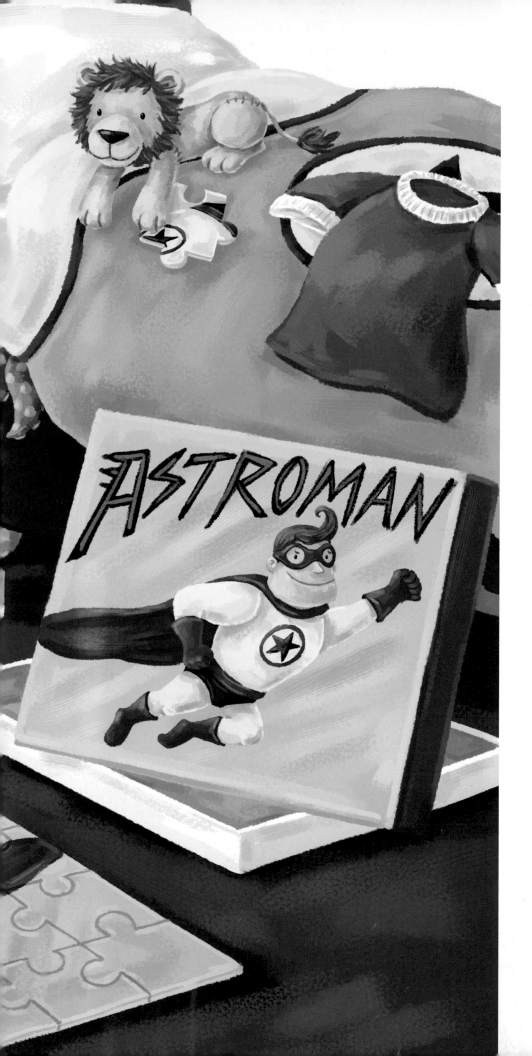

I'm just hunting for the last piece when . . .

"Albie!"

It's Mum.

"Just look at the state of your room!" she says.

"If you can tidy up before this rings,

I'll take you out for ice cream."

Tick.

Tick.

Tick . . .

Quick as a flash, I pull on my cloak and mask.
"This is a job for Albie the Awesome!" I say.

Suddenly . . .

SWOOSH!

Something swoops past me, grabs my last jigsaw piece and dives into the wardrobe! "Hey!" I cry. "That's mine!"
Without thinking, I dive in after them.

AAAHHH!

Down,

down,

down I fall, tumbling through the darkness.

HEEELLLP!

Suddenly, a gloved hand grips mine.
"Got you!"
It's a flying girl!

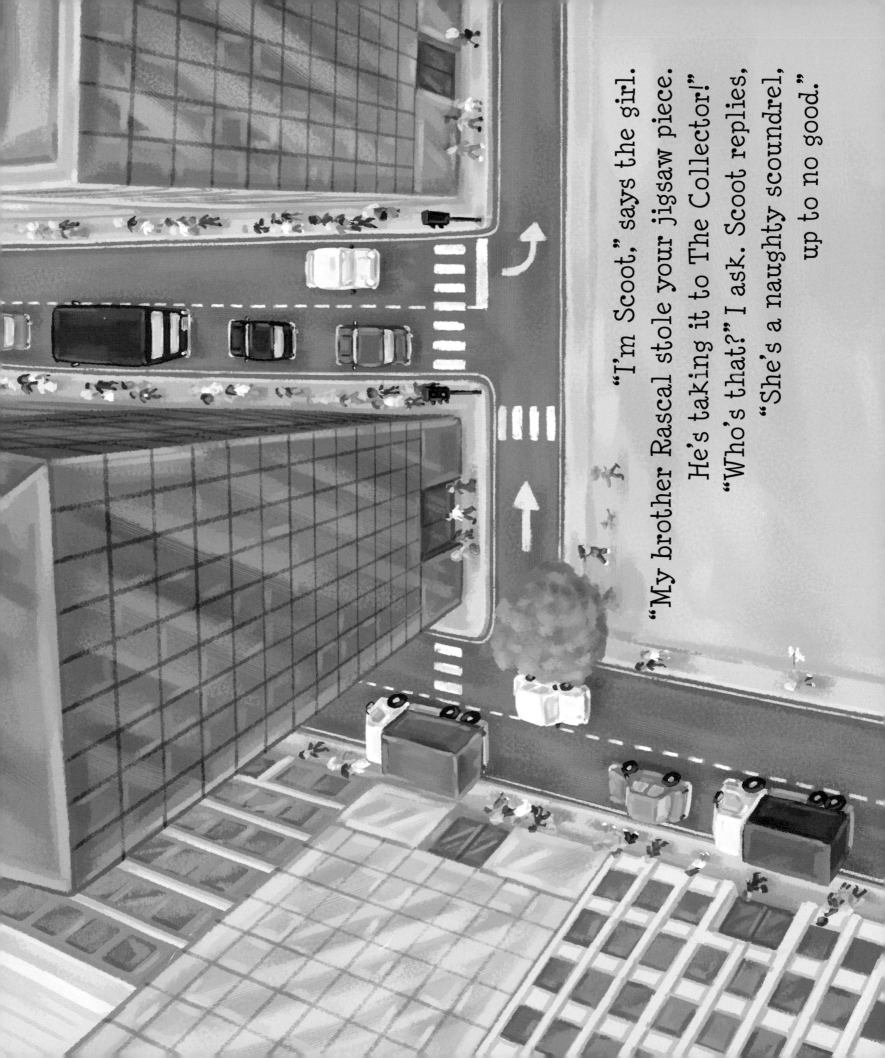

"I'm Scoot," says the girl.
"My brother Rascal stole your jigsaw piece.
He's taking it to The Collector!"
"Who's that?" I ask. Scoot replies,
"She's a naughty scoundrel,
up to no good."

I cling to Scoot's hand as we swoop in and out
of the skyscrapers, far above a busy city.

"There he is!" shouts Scoot. "Rascal! STOP!" But Rascal flies to a tall clock tower and disappears inside!

We peer through a keyhole.
It's The Collector's lair! She snatches
my puzzle piece from Rascal. Uh-oh!

"It's the wrong piece," The Collector scowls.
"Now I'll NEVER finish my masterpiece and
it's all YOUR fault!"

"Please don't be angry," says Rascal. "I thought we were friends."
"Not any more!" growls The Collector. She picks up a pen and
points it at Rascal. "Sweet dreams, sucker!"

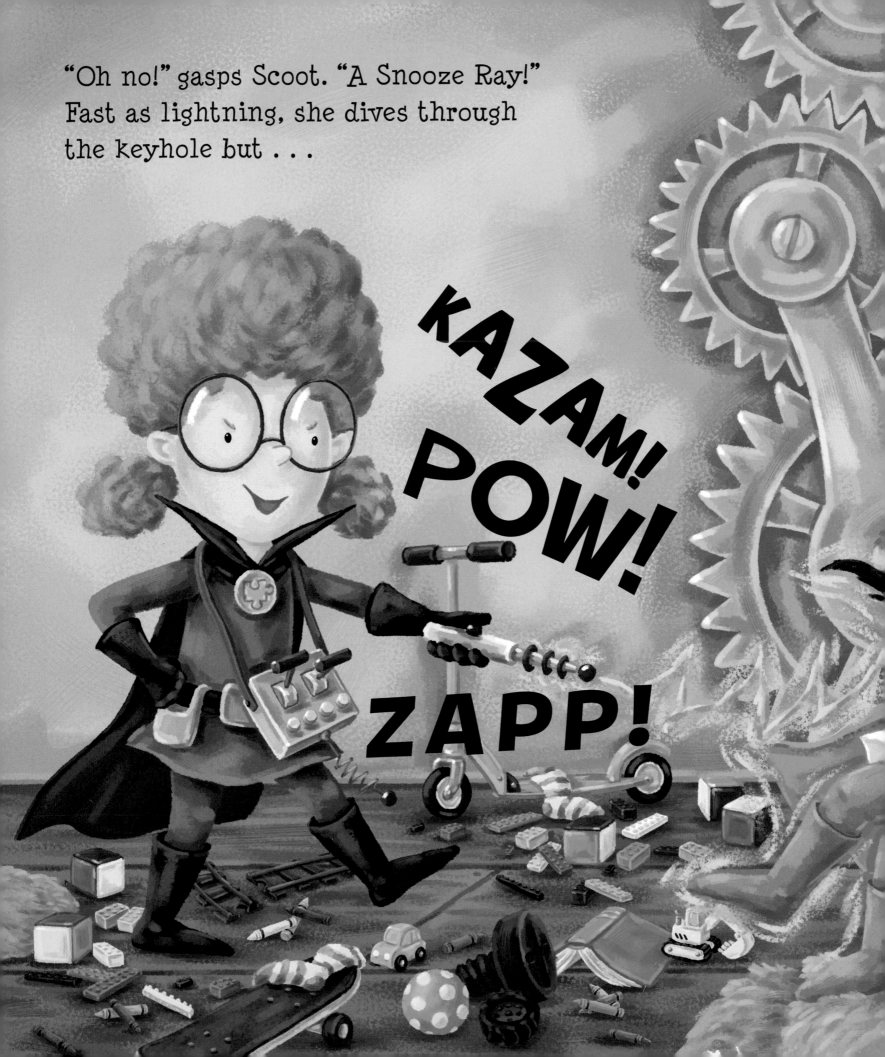

"Oh no!" gasps Scoot. "A Snooze Ray!"
Fast as lightning, she dives through
the keyhole but . . .

The Snooze Ray hits her and she drops to the ground.

Oh no!

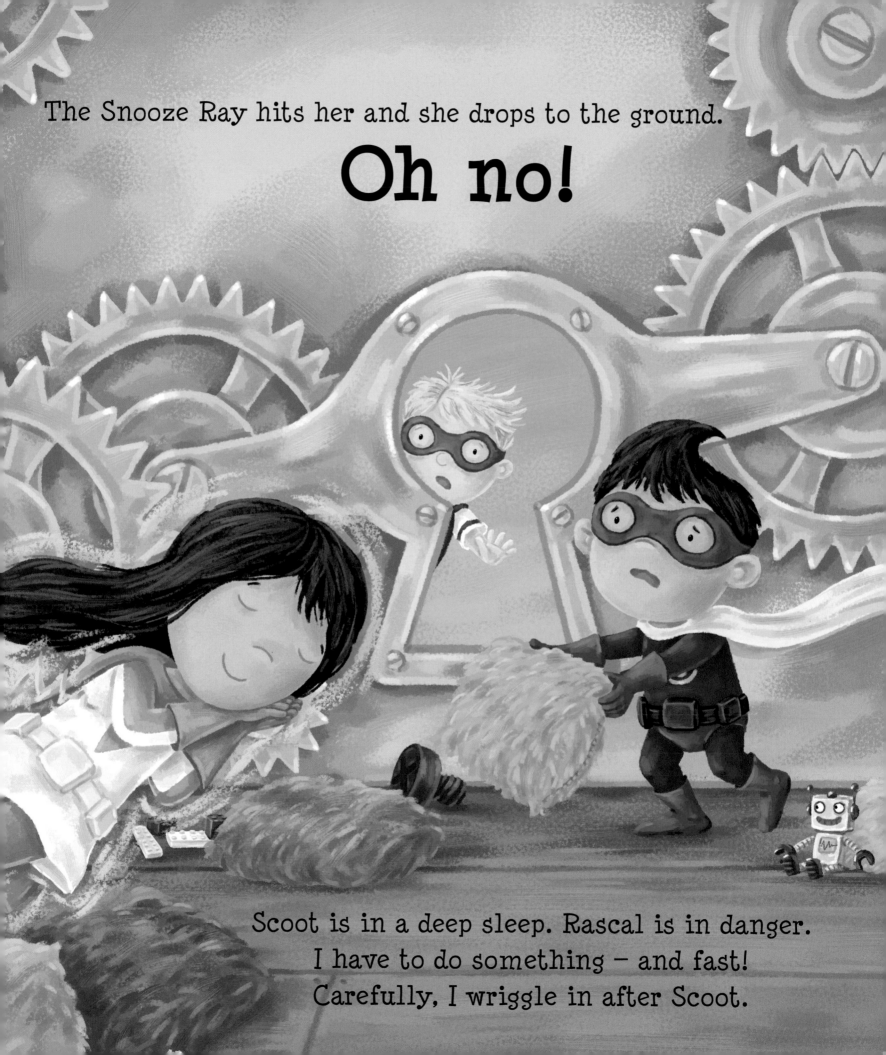

Scoot is in a deep sleep. Rascal is in danger.
I have to do something – and fast!
Carefully, I wriggle in after Scoot.

"Wait!" I say. "The right piece could be here somewhere.
If you un-snooze Scoot, we could all tidy up and find it."

"I don't need your help!" growls The Collector. "Watch this."

She fiddles with her remote control
and the roof opens up!
A strange machine splutters into life.
It sucks up great gulps of toys and
books and puzzles.

WOAH!

Then . . .

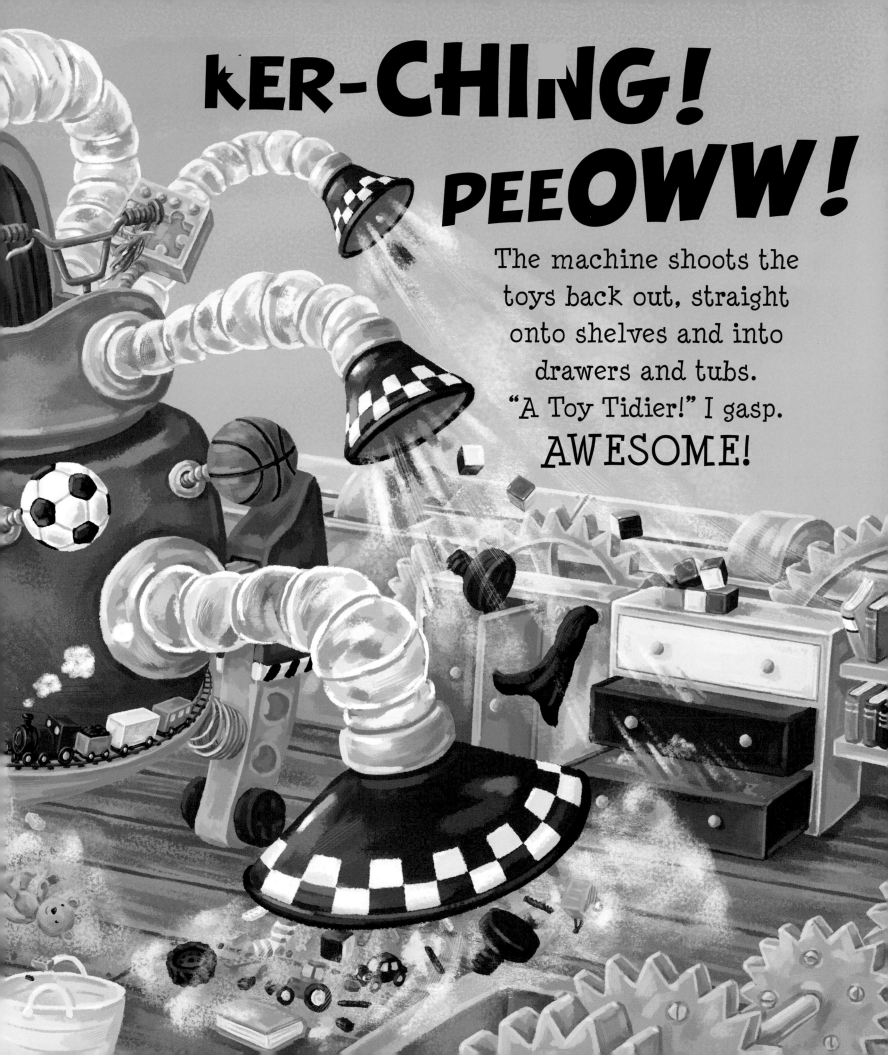

KER-CHING!
PEEOWW!

The machine shoots the toys back out, straight onto shelves and into drawers and tubs. "A Toy Tidier!" I gasp. AWESOME!

"Actually it's a Flying Game Grabber," says The Collector. "But until I find the right piece it will only grab MY toys! A-HA!" she smiles. "This might be it!"

She fits it into the Game Grabber, and it starts to fly! "Now NOBODY will be able to stop me. Soon all the toys in the world will be mine, mine, MINE! MWA-HA-HA-HA-HA!"

Uh-oh!

I leap on board and point the Snooze Ray at her.
"Turn this machine around NOW!" I shout.
"Okay! Okay!" she cries. "Just put that thing down."
When we land, I switch the Snooze Ray into reverse
and point it at Scoot.

MAZAK! WOP! PAZZ!

Scoot jumps to her feet in a fury.

"Don't worry, Albie has saved us!" says Rascal.

The clock chimes **DONG!** Oh no – Mum's timer!
"I've got to go," I gasp. "I'm meant to be tidying my OWN room!"
Rascal and Scoot glare at The Collector. "Well?"

"Oh, all right!" she says.
"I'll help if you let me keep my machine."

HOORAY!

We all jump onto the Flying Game Grabber and head for home.

WHOOSH!

"Come on then," says Scoot.
"Show us what you can do."

WOOOOAAAHHH!

In no time at all, my bedroom is neat and tidy.
YIPPEE!

Just as we finish, Mum opens my bedroom door.
"Wow, Albie," she gasps. "Your room looks amazing."

I smile at my new friends.
"Tidying up is easy when you use your superpowers," I say.

"Well done, Albie the Awesome," smiles
Mum. "Let's go and get that ice cream."

Uh-oh!